Dear Parents:

W9-AES-004

Congratulations! Your child is taking the first steps on an exciting journey. The destination? Independent reading!

STEP INTO READING® will help your child get there. The program offers five steps to reading success. Each step includes fun stories and colorful art or photographs. In addition to original fiction and books with favorite characters, there are Step into Reading Non-Fiction Readers, Phonics Readers and Boxed Sets, Sticker Readers, and Comic Readers—a complete literacy program with something to interest every child.

Learning to Read, Step by Step!

Ready to Read   Preschool–Kindergarten
• big type and easy words • rhyme and rhythm • picture clues
For children who know the alphabet and are eager to begin reading.

Reading with Help   Preschool–Grade 1
• basic vocabulary • short sentences • simple stories
For children who recognize familiar words and sound out new words with help.

Reading on Your Own   Grades 1–3
• engaging characters • easy-to-follow plots • popular topics
For children who are ready to read on their own.

Reading Paragraphs   Grades 2–3
• challenging vocabulary • short paragraphs • exciting stories
For newly independent readers who read simple sentences with confidence.

Ready for Chapters   Grades 2–4
• chapters • longer paragraphs • full-color art
For children who want to take the plunge into chapter books but still like colorful pictures.

STEP INTO READING® is designed to give every child a successful reading experience. The grade levels are only guides; children will progress through the steps at their own speed, developing confidence in their reading.

Remember, a lifetime love of reading starts with a single step!

For Mom, my very best friend
—M.L.

Copyright © 2016 Disney Enterprises, Inc. All rights reserved. Published in the United States by Random House Children's Books, a division of Penguin Random House LLC, 1745 Broadway, New York, NY 10019, and in Canada by Penguin Random House Canada Limited, Toronto, in conjunction with Disney Enterprises, Inc.

Step into Reading, Random House, and the Random House colophon are registered trademarks of Penguin Random House LLC.

Visit us on the Web!
StepIntoReading.com
randomhousekids.com

Educators and librarians, for a variety of teaching tools, visit us at RHTeachersLibrarians.com

ISBN 978-0-7364-3670-0 (trade) — ISBN 978-0-7364-8194-6 (lib. bdg.)
ISBN 978-0-7364-3671-7 (ebook)

Printed in the United States of America   10 9 8 7 6 5 4 3 2 1

Random House Children's Books supports the First Amendment and celebrates the right to read.

DISNEY PRINCESS

Friends for a Princess

by Melissa Lagonegro

illustrated by Atelier Philippe Harchy

Random House 🏠 New York

Snow White has
seven little friends.
Loving, kind,
and special friends.

R0446145321

Some have big beards.

Some have small.

Dopey has

no beard at all.

Doc is caring.

Doc is wise.

Doc needs glasses

for his eyes.

Happy is
a cheerful guy.

Bashful is

so very shy.

Sneezy always
has to sneeze.

Grumpy is
so hard to please.

Sleepy likes

to take a nap.

Dopey wears

a purple cap.

They all dance
through the night.

The Seven Dwarfs
love Snow White.